Mr. Little's NOISY ABC

Richard Fowler

whoops!

clatter!

ABC

Designed and produced by Ventura Publishing Limited,
11–13 Young Street, London W8 5EH, England.
Printed in Singapore.

Aa

"Ahhh!" yells Mr. Little **as** he falls out of the **apple** tree onto the **anthill.**

"Buzz, buzz,"
go the **busy bees** around
Mr. Little's **bun.**

Cc

Crunch!
Mr. Little's **car crashes**
into the **cottage.**

Ding dong, ding dong!
Mr. Little **dangles dangerously**
as he rings the bell.

Ee

"Eeeek!" screams Mr. Little. "There's an **earwig** on my **elbow**!"

Fizz, fizz. The bubbles in the **fruit** punch make Mr. Little **feel funny.**

Gg

"Grrr, grrr," Mr. Little's dog **growls** at a **gopher** in the **grass**.

"Ha, ha, ha,"
hoots Mr. Little dressed up
as a **happy harlequin.**

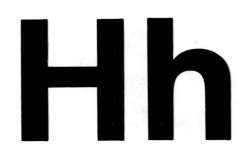

Ii

"**Izzical** whizzical. **I'll** make you **invisible!**" says Mr. Little the **incredible** magician.

Magic Spells **inside**

Jingle jangle. The chains **jump** and **jolt** as Mr. Little drives his **jalopy**.

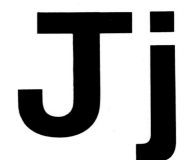

Kk

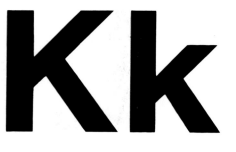

"**Kraak, kraak,**" screeches th
jay as Mr. Little **keeps** flying
his **kite** near the tree.

"La, la, la," sings Mr. **Little** as he **lathers** his **leg** and **lies** back in the bathtub.

Mm

"Moo, moo,"
goes the **moody** cow and
makes Mr. Little **move!**

Natter, natter, natter.
Mr. Little's **noisy neighbors**
never stop **nagging**.

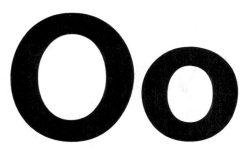

Oo

"**Ow, ow, ow!**" yells Mr. Little as the **oilcan** falls **off** the bench and **onto** his foot!

Plip plop, plip plop.
The rain water **pours** down
the **pipe** and into the **puddle**.

Qq

"Quack, quack, quack." The **quarrelsome** ducks disturb Mr. Little's **quiet** afternoon.

Rat-a-tat-tat!
Mr. Little **raps** on the **red**
door of the **restaurant**.

Ss

Sizzle, sizzle.
Mr. Little's **saucepan** of **stew** goes up in **smoke!**

Tick tock, tick tock. The **tall** grandfather clock **tells** Mr. Little it's **time to** get up!

Tt

Uu

"Ugh!" Mr. Little **uncovers** an **ugly** insect in the **undergrowth.**

Vroom, vroom!
Mr. Little's **very** fast **vehicle**
veers off the track.

Ww

Whoosh!
The **wild wind** blows
Mr. Little's **window** open.

Xing xang xong!
Mr. Little excels at
xylophone playing!

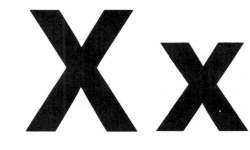

Yy

"Yap, yap!"
The **yellow** dog chases
Mr. Little around the **yard**!

2-14-87

my Mom —
a sweet tribute to
others and motherhood f...
wonderful mom. You've been...
example and inspiration to me a...
...ived what loving is all about. Happy
Valentines Day. I love you.

Jut

A
Mother's Posy

edited by

CELIA HADDON

MICHAEL JOSEPH
LONDON

To My Sister

First published in Great Britain by
Michael Joseph Ltd
44 Bedford Square, London WC1
May 1982

ISBN 0 7181 2143 0

Designed by Penny Mills

Printed and bound in Singapore

Also by Celia Haddon
A CHRISTMAS POSY
A LOVER'S POSY

[2]

CONTENTS

His Majesty The Baby

His eyes of clear and cloudless brown,
His hair a soft and silky down,
His face the sweetest, all must own:
You recognise him, maybe?
We know but one such words could suit,
But one whose will is past dispute,
Whose sovreign law is absolute:
His Majesty the Baby.

No mightier monarch e'er was known,
His right divine we gladly own,
For it is based on love alone:
A right which knows no maybe.
A sceptre this we gladly kiss,
And own our saddest moment this:
When for the briefest space we miss
His Majesty the Baby!

We know not what before him lies,
What shall await him – smiles or sighs,
A stormy path, or sunny skies:
These things may not or may be.
Whate'er the great Unknown shall bring,
We fear it not while we can sing
With trustful hearts, God Save Our King,
His Majesty the Baby.

A. CHARLES HAMILTON

A happy new year

A Baby's Hands

A baby's hands, like rosebuds furled
Whence yet no leaf expands,
Ope if you touch, though close upcurled,
A baby's hands.

Then, fast as warriors grip their brands
When battle's bolt is hurled,
They close, clenched hard like tightening bands.

No rosebuds yet by dawn impearled
Match, even in loveliest lands,
The sweetest flowers in all the world –
A baby's hands.

ALGERNON CHARLES SWINBURNE

A VERY HAPPY SEASON to you!

MAY THE COMING SEASON BRING
JOY AND GLADNESS ON ITS WING.

A Baby's Feet

A baby's feet, like sea-shells pink,
Might tempt, should heaven see meet,
An angel's lips to kiss, we think,
A baby's feet.

Like rose-hued sea-flowers toward the heat
They stretch and spread and wink
Their ten soft buds that part and meet.

No flower-bells that expand and shrink
Gleam half so heavenly sweet
As shine on life's untrodden brink
A baby's feet.

ALGERNON CHARLES SWINBURNE

A GRACE

Here a little child I stand
Heaving up my either hand;
Cold as paddocks though they be,
Here I lift them up to Thee,
For a benison to fall
On our meat and on us all.

ROBERT HERRICK

UPON THY PATH MAY HEAVENLY SUNBEAMS PLAY,
AND BRING TO THEE A MERRY CHRISTMAS DAY.

My Baby

My baby has a mottled fist,
My baby has a neck in creases;
My baby kisses and is kissed,
For he's the very thing for kisses.

CHRISTINA ROSSETTI

Wishing you many Happy Returns.

FROM Frost At Midnight

Dear Babe, that sleepest cradled by my side,
Whose gentle breathings, heard in this deep calm,
Fill up the interspersed vacancies
And momentary pauses of the thought!
My babe so beautiful! it thrills my heart
With tender gladness, thus to look at thee,
And think that thou shalt learn far other lore,
And in far other scenes! For I was reared
In the great city, pent 'mid cloisters dim,
And saw nought lovely but the sky and stars.
But *thou*, my babe! shalt wander like a breeze
By lakes and sandy shores, beneath the crags
Of ancient mountain, and beneath the clouds,
Which image in their bulk both lakes and shores
And mountain crags: so shalt thou see and hear
The lovely shapes and sounds intelligible
Of that eternal language, which thy God
Utters, who from eternity doth teach
Himself in all, and all things in himself. . . .
Therefore all seasons shall be sweet to thee,
Whether the summer clothe the general earth
With greenness, or the redbreast sit and sing
Betwixt the tufts of snow on the bare branch
Of mossy apple-tree, while the nigh thatch
Smokes in the sun-thaw; whether the eave-drops fall
Heard only in the trances of the blast,
Or if the secret ministry of frost
Shall hang them up in silent icicles,
Quietly shining to the quiet Moon.

SAMUEL TAYLOR COLERIDGE

THE TOYS

My little Son, who look'd from thoughtful eyes
And moved and spoke in quiet grown-up wise,
Having my law the seventh time disobey'd,
I struck him, and dismiss'd
With hard words and unkiss'd,
His Mother, who was patient, being dead.
Then, fearing lest his grief should hinder sleep,
I visited his bed,
But found him slumbering deep,
With darken'd eyelids, and their lashes yet
From his late sobbing wet.
And I, with moan,
Kissing away his tears, left others of my own;
For, on a table drawn beside his head,
He had put, within his reach,
A box of counters and a red-vein'd stone,
A piece of glass abraded by the beach
And six or seven shells,
A box with bluebells
And two French copper coins, ranged there with careful art,
To comfort his sad heart.
So when that night I pray'd
To God, I wept and said:
"Ah, when at last we lie with tranced breath,
Not vexing Thee in death,
And Thou rememberest of what toys
We made our joys. . . .
Thou'lt leave Thy wrath, and say,
'I will be sorry for their childishness.' "

COVENTRY PATMORE

New Prince, New Pomp

Behold a silly tender Babe,
   In freezing winter night,
   In homely manger trembling lies;
   Alas! a piteous sight.
The inns are full, no man will yield
   This little Pilgrim bed;
   But forced He is with silly beasts,
   In crib to shroud His head.
Despise Him not for lying here,
   First what He is inquire:
   An orient pearl is often found
   In depth of dirty mire.
Weigh not His crib, His wooden dish,
   Nor beasts that by Him feed:
   Weigh not His mother's poor attire,
   Nor Joseph's simple weed.
This stable is a Prince's court,
   The crib His chair of state;
   The beasts are parcel of His pomp,
   The wooden dish His plate;
The persons in that poor attire,
   His royal liveries wear;
   The Prince himself is come from Heaven,
   This pomp is prizèd there.

ROBERT SOUTHWELL

Behold, what manner of love the Father hath bestowed upon us, that we should be called the sons of God.

1 John 3: 1.

C-863

IF MOTHER KNEW

If mother knew the way I felt –
And I'm sure a mother should –
She wouldn't make it quite so hard
For a person to be good!

I want to do the things she says;
I try to all day long;
And then she just skips all the right,
And pounces on the wrong.

A dozen times I do a thing,
And one time I forget;
And then she looks at me and asks
If I can't remember yet?

I wonder if she really thinks
A child could go so far,
As to be perfect all the time
As the grown-up people are!

If she only knew I tried to –
And I'm sure a mother should –
She wouldn't make it quite so hard
For a person to be good.

ANONYMOUS

PEACE
ON
EARTH

A happy Christmas

INTIMATIONS OF IMMORTALITY

FROM RECOLLECTIONS OF EARLY CHILDHOOD

Our birth is but a sleep and a forgetting:
The Soul that rises with us, our life's Star,
    Hath had elsewhere its setting,
      And cometh from afar:
    Not in entire forgetfulness,
    And not in utter nakedness,
But trailing clouds of glory do we come
    From God, who is our home:
Heaven lies about us in our infancy!
Shades of the prison-house begin to close
    Upon the growing Boy,
But He beholds the light, and whence it flows,
    He sees it in his joy;
The Youth, who daily farther from the East
    Must travel, still is Nature's Priest,
    And by the vision splendid
    Is on his way attended;
At length the Man perceives it die away,
And fade into the light of common day.

Earth fills her lap with pleasures of her own;
Yearnings she hath in her own natural kind,
And, even with something of a Mother's mind,
    And no unworthy aim,
    The homely Nurse doth all she can
To make her Foster-child, her Inmate Man
    Forget the glories he hath known
And that imperial palace whence he came.

Behold the Child among his new-born Blisses,
A six years' Darling of a pigmy size!
See, where mid work of his own hand he lies,
Fretted by sallies of his Mother's kisses,
With light upon him from his Father's eyes!
See, at his feet, some little plan or chart,
Some fragment from his dream of human life,
Shap'd by himself with newly-learned art;
    A wedding or a festival,
    A mourning or a funeral;
      And this hath now his heart,
    And unto this he frames his song:
      Then will he fit his tongue
To dialogues of business, love, or strife;
    But it will not be long
    Ere this be thrown aside,
    And with new joy and pride
The little Actor cons another part,
Filling from time to time his 'humorous stage'
With all the Persons, down to palsied Age,
That Life brings with her in her Equipage;
    And if his whole vocation
    Were endless imitation. . . .

WILLIAM WORDSWORTH

Of My Dear Son Gervase Beaumont

Dear Lord, receive my son, whose winning love
To me was like a friendship, far above
The course of nature, or his tender age,
Whose looks could all my bitter griefs assuage.

Let his pure soul, ordained seven years to be
In that frail body, which was part of me,
Remain my pledge in heaven, as sent to show
How to this port at every step I go.

JOHN BEAUMONT

FAVOURITES

PLEASURES

My daughter loves the light
For its own sake, innocent
Of what it may illuminate;
The sun floods her eyes
With free gold and we
Brighten the fire to please her.
Later she may care to see
The roses feeding
On soil and crystal air
But they will die
Inviolate before she knows them better.
The light will always be
Her agent and her friend
But she will write her own shadows
With an early hand.

PHILIP OAKES

The Blind Boy

O say, what is that thing called light,
What I can ne'er enjoy?
What is the blessing of the sight?
O tell your poor blind boy!

You talk of wondrous things you see,
You say the sun shines bright;
I feel him warm, but how can he
Then make it day or night?

My day or night myself I make
Whene'er I sleep or play;
And could I ever keep awake
With me 'twere always day.

With heavy sighs I often hear
You mourn my hapless woe;
But sure with patience I may bear
A loss I ne'er can know.

Then let not what I cannot have
My cheer of mind destroy;
Whilst thus I sing, I am a king,
Although a poor blind boy.

COLLEY CIBBER

On the Picture of a Sleeping Child

Sweet babe, whose image here expressed
Does thy peaceful slumbers show;
Guilt or fear, to break thy rest,
Never did thy spirit know.

Soothing slumbers, soft repose,
Such as mock the painter's skill,
Such as innocence bestows,
Harmless infant, lull thee still!

WILLIAM COWPER

THE LAMB

Little lamb, who made thee?
Dost thou know who made thee?
Gave thee life, and bid thee feed
By the stream and o'er the mead;
Gave thee clothing of delight,
Softest clothing, woolly, bright;
Gave thee such a tender voice,
Making all the vales rejoice?
Little lamb, who made thee?
Dost thou know who made thee?

Little lamb, I'll tell thee,
Little lamb, I'll tell thee:
He is callèd by thy name,
For he calls himself a lamb.
He is meek, and he is mild;
He became a little child.
I a child, and thou a lamb,
We are callèd by his name.
Little lamb, God bless thee!
Little lamb, God bless thee!

WILLIAM BLAKE

[29]

Marion's Baby

There he lay upon his back,
The yearling creature, warm and moist with life
To the bottom of his dimples, – and to the ends
Of the lovely tumbled curls about his face;
For since he had been covered over-much
To keep him from the light-glare, both his cheeks
Were hot and scarlet as the first live rose
The shepherd's heart-blood ebbed away into
The faster for his love. And love was here
As instant; in the pretty baby-mouth,
Shut close as if for dreaming that it sucked,
The little naked feet, drawn up the way
Of nestled birdlings; everything so soft
And tender – to the tiny holdfast hands
Which, closing on a finger into sleep,
Had kept a mould of't.

ELIZABETH BARRETT BROWNING

Parental Recollections

A child's a plaything for an hour;
Its pretty tricks we try
For that, or for a longer space;
Then tire, and lay it by.

But I knew one, that to itself
All seasons could control;
That would have mock'd the sense of pain
Out of a grieved soul.

Thou, straggler into loving arms,
Young climber-up of knees,
When I forget thy thousand ways
Then life and all shall cease.

MARY LAMB

A Merry Xmas and a Happy New Year.

A Father's Lullaby

'Lullaby, oh, lullaby!'
Thus I heard a father cry,
'Lullaby, oh, lullaby!
The brat will never shut an eye;
Hither come, some power divine!
Close his lids or open mine!

'Lullaby, oh, lullaby!
What the devil makes him cry?
Lullaby, oh, lullaby!
Still he stares – I wonder why?
Why are not the sons of earth
Blind, like puppies, from the birth?

'Lullaby, oh, lullaby!'
Thus I heard the father cry;
'Lullaby, oh, lullaby!
Mary, you must come and try! –
Hush, oh, hush, for mercy's sake –
The more I sing, the more you wake!

'Lullaby, oh, lullaby!
Two such nights, and I shall die!
Lullaby, oh, lullaby!
He'll be bruised, and so shall I, –
How can I from bedposts keep,
When I'm walking in my sleep?'

THOMAS HOOD

[35]

A Happy

BIRTHDAY to my darling!

The Little People

A dreary place would this earth be
Were there no little people in it;
The song of life would lose its mirth,
Were there no children to begin it;

No forms, like buds to grow,
And make the admiring heart surrender;
No little hands on breast and brow,
To keep the thrilling love-chords tender.

The sterner souls would grow more stern,
Unfeeling nature more inhuman,
And man to stoic coldness turn,
And woman would be less than woman.

Life's song, indeed, would lose its charm,
Were there no babies to begin it;
A doleful place this world would be,
Were there no little people in it.

J.G. WHITTIER

The Children's Hour

Between the dark and the daylight,
When the night is beginning to lower,
Comes a pause in the day's occupations
That is known as the Children's Hour.

I hear in the chamber above me
The patter of little feet,
The sound of a door that is open'd,
And voices soft and sweet.

From my study I see in the lamplight,
Descending the broad hall stair,
Grave Alice and laughing Allegra,
And Edith with golden hair.

A whisper and then a silence:
Yet I know by their merry eyes
They are plotting and planning together
To take me by surprise.

A sudden rush from the stairway,
A sudden raid from the hall!
By three doors left unguarded
They enter my castle wall.

HENRY WADSWORTH LONGFELLOW

HAPPY NEW YEAR TO MY DEAR LITTLE FRIEND

The Land of Counterpane

When I was sick and lay a-bed,
I had two pillows at my head,
And all my toys beside me lay
To keep me happy all the day.

And sometimes for an hour or so
I watched my leaden soldiers go,
With different uniforms and drills,
Among the bedclothes, through the hills;

And sometimes sent my ships in fleets
All up and down among the sheets;
Or brought my trees and houses out,
And planted cities all about.

I was the giant great and still
That sits upon the pillow-hill,
And sees before him, dale and plain,
The pleasant land of counterpane.

ROBERT LOUIS STEVENSON

The Little Black Boy

My mother bore me in the southern wild,
And I am black, but O my soul is white!
White as an angel is the English child,
But I am black, as if bereaved of light.

My mother taught me underneath a tree,
And sitting down before the heat of day,
She took me on her lap and kissed me,
And pointing to the east, began to say:

'Look on the rising sun: there God does live,
And gives his light, and gives his heat away;
And flowers and trees and beasts and men receive
Comfort in morning, joy in the noonday.

'And we are put on earth a little space,
That we may learn to bear the beams of love;
And these black bodies and this sunburnt face
Is but a cloud, and like a shady grove.

'For when our souls have learned the heat to bear,
The cloud will vanish; we shall hear his voice,
Saying, "Come out from the grove, my love and care,
And round my golden tent like lambs rejoice. . . ." '

WILLIAM BLAKE

I Know A Baby

I know a baby, such a baby, –
Round blue eyes and cheeks of pink,
Such an elbow furrowed with dimples,
Such a wrist where creases sink.

'Cuddle and love me, cuddle and love me,'
Crows the mouth of coral pink:
Oh the bald head, and oh the sweet lips,
And oh the sleepy eyes that wink!

CHRISTINA ROSSETTI

MY MOTHER.

MY MOTHER

Who fed me from her gentle breast,
And hushed me in her arms to rest,
And on my cheek sweet kisses pressed?
        My mother.

When sleep forsook my open eye,
Who was it sung sweet hushaby,
And rocked me that I should not cry?
        My mother.

Who dressed my doll in clothes so gay,
And fondly taught me how to play,
And minded all I had to say?
        My mother.

Who ran to help me when I fell,
And would some pretty story tell,
Or kiss the place to make it well?
        My mother.

And can I ever cease to be
Affectionate and kind to thee,
Who was so very kind to me,
        My mother?

ANN TAYLOR

The editor wishes to express gratitude to The
Mansell Collection and to the Mary Evans Picture
Library for pictures reproduced in this book.